Naomi's Road

— Joy Kogawa —

Drawings by Ruth Ohi

Fitzhenry & Whiteside

First published by Fitzhenry & Whiteside in 2005
First published by Oxford University Press in 1986

Published in Canada by Fitzhenry & Whiteside, 195 Allstate Parkway, Markham, Ontario L3R 4T8

www.fitzhenry.ca   godwit@fitzhenry.ca

10 9 8 7 6 5 4 3 2 1

Library and Archives Canada Cataloguing in Publication
Kogawa, Joy
      Naomi's road / Joy Kogawa ; [illustrations by] Ruth Ohi.

An adaptation for children of the author's novel Obasan.
For 6-8 year olds.
ISBN 1-55005-115-6

      1. Japanese Canadians—Evacuation and relocation, 1942-1945—Juvenile fiction.
I. Ohi, Ruth II. Title.

PS8521.O44N36 2005   jC813'.54
C2005-900061-9

Fitzhenry & Whiteside acknowledges with thanks the Canada Council for the Arts, the Government of Canada through the Book Publishing Industry Development Program (BPIDP), and the Ontario Arts Council for their support of our publishing program.

Design by Christine Toller
Printed and bound in Canada

For Matthew and Anne

J.K.

Note on this Edition

This new edition of *Naomi's Road* is based on *Naomi-no-Michi*, an expanded version that was translated by Michiko Asami and published in Japan.

Acknowledgements

Grateful thanks to the Kogawa Homestead Committee—Margaret Steffler, Roy Miki, Sook C. Kong, Keiko Miki, Lois Wilson, Daphne Marlatt, Steve Turnbull, Tracy Matsuo, David Kogawa, Timothy Nakayama, Linda Ohama, Stephanie Gould, Ann-Marie Metten—and especially Anton Wagner and Chris Kurata, for valiant efforts on behalf of the house and the cherry tree at 1450 West 64th Avenue in Vancouver, B.C. Thanks also to Lucy Meyer, the real estate agent, for understanding my love of the house; and to Arlene Lampert, Ian Sowton, Lee Davis Creal and Christianne Hayward and the Chronicle Crusaders for their comments.

Special thanks to Ann Featherstone for patient and careful editorial work, and to Gail Winskill and Sharon Fitzhenry for believing in this edition.

Most of all, thank you to my children, Gordon and Deidre, whose love sustains me.

Chapter 1

Bong, bong, bong.... Five, six, seven. Evening's shadowy light is soft and quiet. The mantel clock in the living room chimes that it's bath time at Naomi's house.

Grandma Kato is waiting in the hot, hot water, for four-year-old Naomi, the youngest in the family.

"Come," Grandma Kato calls. She is sweating in the misty steam.

When Naomi steps in, Grandma Kato sits up and moves to the tap end. The fierce water hurts, but Grandma is happy that Naomi is brave. Naomi's feet turn lobster red, as if she were wearing red socks.

"Cold, cold," Grandma says, laughing. Naomi is braver than her big seven-year-old brother Stephen. He won't go into such angry water.

Naomi sits slowly, carefully, while Grandma Kato lies down again. "Ah...," Grandma says and closes her eyes. Naomi finally gets all covered in the hot water up to her neck, and she is comfortable. After they soak, Grandma scrubs Naomi with her wash cloth rolled tight as a fist.

Grandma Kato is so bony and tough Naomi thinks she could sit in a boiling pot on a stove and not be cooked. She's the toughest woman in the world. She has bony knees and bony hands and a thin face, and the only time she seems to rest is when she takes a bath.

When the bath is over, Naomi walks sleepily to get a tea biscuit and then goes into the sunroom. She is in her *nemaki*, her Japanese nightie, which is like a cotton housecoat with a tie. She curls up round as a peach in the big bamboo wing chair. The air is bouncing cheerfully with the easy pieces Mama and Stephen are playing. Mama's buckled shoe taps against the piano stool's skinny legs. *Tap, tap.* If Stephen makes a mistake, he shakes his head, pushes his round glasses back up his nose and frowns. Behind them, Daddy bobs up and down like a dancer.

"And one, and two, up'n one, and two…"

Daddy's long fingers hold a pencil, which makes squiggly marks on Stephen's music book.

Naomi dreamily munches her biscuit and watches the two fat goldfish in the bowl near the window ledge, swimming back and forth, opening their hungry mouths.

Mama's voice, singing Naomi's kindergarten song, is *yasashi*—soft and tender. Mama is always *yasashi*. She's trying to coax Naomi to join them, but Naomi is too lazy after the bath.

How did you, Miss Daffodilly,
Get your pretty dress?
Is it made of gold and sunshine?
Yes, child, yes.

"Mmm. Your biscuit looks good," Daddy says, coming over and pretending he's a goldfish smacking its lips.

"Silly," Naomi giggles. She breaks off a piece for him.

Beside the goldfish bowl is a porcelain statue of a young Japanese man. Naomi slides her hand over his hard, shiny head, over the lump of twigs on his back and down to the shiny book in the shiny little hands.

"See how he carries the wood?" Daddy asks. "See

his book?" He lifts the heavy statue and places it carefully in Naomi's hands.

Stephen stops playing the piano and comes over to listen.

"Nee-no mee-ya Keen-jeero," Daddy says slowly. "Can you say his name, Naomi? He was a poor boy. A poor, poor boy. Imagine a life with no food. No? You can't imagine it? Nino-miya Kin-jiro had a baby brother and a mother, and they had no food. He used to get up early every morning in the dark, before the rooster crowed. And away he'd go, into the mountains to gather wood to sell. But do you see what's in his hands? A book! He loved books. He loved to feel them and smell them. He read them all by himself as he walked. And do you know what? He became the greatest teacher in all Japan."

Daddy takes the figure and rubs its smooth cold cheek against Stephen's and Naomi's cheeks. "That's because he studied by himself. All by himself. Nobody helped him. He was so lucky because he loved books. He had a special road. The road of learning. Everyone has a special road. You do, Stephen. And so do you, Naomi."

Mama stops playing the kindergarten songs. "Yes," she says, "we all learn what our road is some day."

"What's yours, Mama?" Naomi asks.

Mama takes Naomi's hand. "I think my road has something to do with N and S," she says, "That's a riddle for you. N and S. My special N and my special S."

"Oh, that's easy. N and S. That's North and South," Daddy says.

"Wrong!" Mama says.

"Hmm," Stephen says. "N must stand for Ninny, Nonny, Noony."

Mama laughs and pats Stephen's cheek. "Well, time for bed." She takes Naomi's hand and off they go over the deep blue Indian rug and through the living room, the darkest room, with dim lights on the walls. Sometimes when Naomi and Stephen play with his toy cars, they use the rug's border for roads. And Stephen's lead soldiers, with their bright red coats, march along the lines.

Past the living room, past the dining room with its heavy walnut table, is Naomi's bedroom. Long, white lace curtains over the window reach to the floor. The top of the peach tree almost touches the window. In the back of the yard grows Naomi's favourite tree, the beautiful cherry tree. Just this afternoon Naomi reached the lowest branch and she hung upside down by her arms and legs like a monkey. She could see the bees and butterflies that came to taste the white cherry blossoms, and the birds that were carrying twigs to make a nest. Once, when the window of her bedroom was open, a robin came and landed on the window ledge. It didn't fly away but looked right at Naomi with its bright, curious eye.

Above Naomi's bed is a picture of a little green bird in a green tree. The sky is green too. A little girl with a green book on her lap is looking up at the bird in the tree.

Naomi goes to her window and waves.

"Goodnight, world," she says. "Goodnight, birds and cherry tree."

Chapter 2

"Where are we going?" Naomi asks. "Why are we all dressed up?"

Four grandparents, two aunts and an uncle—the whole big family is having a picture taken today at the photo studio.

"Ten people," Naomi counts, pointing to each one.

"It's eleven, dopey," Stephen says. "You didn't count yourself."

Mama has picked out a pink silk dress and shiny black shoes for Naomi. Stephen is in his short grey pants and suit top, his knee socks and black boots.

Grandma Kato hangs a heavy, sparkling necklace around Naomi's neck. "Crystal for a special day," she says.

The photographer pulls up the chairs. Doctor Kato, Mama's father, sits first. His feet don't reach the floor and the toes of his black boots point down like a ballet dancer. Beside him, stiff and thin in her dark dress is bony Grandma Kato. Next, smiling gently all the time, is round-faced Grandma Nakane, her plump hands in her soft lap. Grandpa Nakane has a droopy moustache. Grandma Nakane helps him, holding his chair steady as he sits down. *Whump!*

Aunt Emily, in her thick glasses, and the rest of the adults cluster together in the back row. Mama's beautiful face is as oval as an egg. She too wears a crystal necklace.

"Now then, you two important people," the photographer says to Naomi and Stephen, pulling up two little velvet stools.

He disappears behind the black cloth. "Still as posts, everyone. Hold still, hold still," he says, holding up his hand.

"Ha," Grandpa Kato says when it is over. "We live again."

Stephen and Naomi take Grandpa Nakane's hands and help him to stand up.

"Stanley Park next," Stephen calls excitedly. This is going to be a day to remember. Everyone loves

Stanley Park, with its giant trees and animals and beaches.

When they arrive, Stephen and Naomi help Grandpa Nakane again as he bends forward to get out of the car. His right arm dangles loosely from his shoulder, close to his knees. It's the way the monkeys walk at the Stanley Park Zoo. Naomi puts potato chips, one by one from her cardboard basket, into Grandpa Nakane's mouth. Grandma Nakane chuckles and says Grandpa Nakane is a good pet for the children.

At the beach, Stephen and Naomi fill their red and blue tin pails with damp sand and dump them upside down to build castles. White pebbles and shells make paths. They wade with Grandpa Nakane along the edge of the cool waves that tickle their feet. After their picnic supper, the outdoor symphony concert begins. This is Stephen's favourite thing—sitting on their blanket on the grass, listening to the music of the world.

Naomi's favourite thing is Christmas and singing carols and riding up and down on the escalators in Woodward's Department Store. In the store windows are a big Snow White doll and the seven dwarves—their pick-axes moving, the music playing, *Hi ho, hi ho, It's off to work we go.*

But for Naomi, the very most favourite thing of all is hearing the stories that Mama tells her every night. Sometimes Mama reads from Naomi's picture books. After that, Naomi always asks Mama to tell the stories about dear old people, which Grandma Kato told Mama when she was a little girl.

"Momotaro. Tell me Momotaro," Naomi says. Over and over every night she hears the same, happy Momotaro story.

Mama lies down on the bed beside her and Naomi snuggles up close to her mother's face. She can smell the sweet powder that Mama pats on her cheeks and neck with her powder puff.

"*Mukaa-shi, mukaa-shi,*" Mama begins, "a long, long time ago, there was an old, old man and an old, old woman who lived in a little cottage in the forest. They were so dear but so lonely because they had no children. 'Little children are more special and more precious than anything in the world,' the old woman sighed. 'Oh, if only there was a little child for us.'

Then one day, when the old, old woman was washing clothes, she saw a huge golden peach rumbling and tumbling down the stream.

"Ah, and what do you think was in the peach?" Mama asks Naomi.

Naomi smiles to herself every time Mama asks this. Naomi is happy thinking of the beautiful baby peach boy, Momotaro, hidden in the middle of a giant peach. She hugs Mama and they sing the peach boy song together. *Momotaro, Momotaro, Momotaro-san...*

Naomi wishes she could have a peach baby. But even if she can't, she thinks she is the luckiest child alive. Her mama is the best mother in the whole world. Her family is the best family that ever was. She wishes she could be a little child forever and forever, just as she is in the family photograph. But children grow up.

"That's the way it goes," Stephen says.

Chapter 3

The small green peaches on the tree outside Naomi's window are the size of Stephen's marbles at first. Daddy says they will eat them when the peaches are as big as Naomi's bouncing ball.

One afternoon, when some of the peaches are almost ready to pick, Naomi is playing with her dolls by the window. Naomi has a teddy bear and a mouse, a nurse doll and her favourite Japanese baby doll. The doll has tiny red lips with two little teeth. Her hair is just like Naomi's—short with straight bangs. She has an orange-coloured tea set with flat light spoons and a tin stove with a tin kettle full of water. The mouse is singing a mouse song when Ralph, the big boy who lives down the alley, comes to play. He's looking for Stephen.

"What are you doing?" he asks. He sits down

on the floor and picks up Naomi's stove. "Want your kettle to boil?" Ralph takes a box of matches from his pocket.

Naomi has never made a fire before. Ralph takes out a match and shows Naomi how to swish it against the side of the box. The fire is so sudden and so hot that she drops the match. Then—surprise! A swift curl of fire runs along the edge of the lace curtain. The fire leaps and flies upward. It's as fast as a bird flying out of a bush.

"Oh-oh!" Ralph shouts. He sounds afraid. "Look what you did, Naomi!" He runs out of the room. "You'll get a spanking."

Naomi stands for a moment watching the curtain burning. Her mama and daddy never spank her or Stephen. The fire catches the other curtain and the flames rush to the window top.

Mama is outside. She will know what to do. Naomi runs to the kitchen door and calls her.

"Mama!"

Mama comes quickly. Bits of burning curtains are dropping through the air. Mama doesn't shout like Ralph did, but runs back and forth with water from the kitchen. And there, on the floor, the dots of fire turn into soggy puddles.

When it's over, Mama and Naomi sit down on the bed and look at the round black spot on the ceiling.

"What happened?" Mama asks quietly.

The burnt match on the floor is shrivelled and black. It crumbles as Naomi picks it up.

"Dangerous, isn't it?" Mama says. Her voice is *yasashi*. Naomi is glad Mama is not afraid like Ralph was. Because Mama isn't afraid, Naomi is not afraid either.

"A match is safe if you know how to blow it out," Mama says. Everything is safe where Mama is, Naomi thinks. Naomi sits close to her, the safest place in the world.

One day, Mama and Grandma Kato are packing to go away. Naomi's great-grandmother in Japan is sick. Mama beckons when she sees Naomi standing in the doorway, watching.

"Can I go with you?" Naomi asks as she helps her mother pack.

Mama takes her crystal necklace off and puts it around Naomi's neck. "Another time," Mama says, straightening the necklace.

"Will you be back for my birthday?" Naomi asks. Naomi is going to be six soon, and then she will be able to go to school.

Mama nods. "Obasan will take care of you. And you'll take care of Obasan, won't you?" she says. "Obasan will make lots of *onigiri*." Obasan is Uncle's wife. She makes *onigiri* rice balls, with salty red plums in the middle.

The day Mama and Grandma go away, it's bright and sunshiny. Everyone is down by the sea where the big boats are. Streamers and streamers are everywhere. The pink, yellow and blue ribbons of paper twirl and sway through the noisy air. It's like a giant maypole dance. Once, when Naomi was very little, she ran into a maypole dance to find Mama but got caught in the streamers. Today Mama is nowhere.

But Obasan is here, and Aunt Emily, Grandpa Kato, Uncle, Daddy and Grandma and Grandpa Nakane. The whole family. Naomi is wearing the blue woollen knit dress that Mama made and likes best. It has white woollen flowers with red-dot centres all around the bottom of the skirt.

"Mama and Grandma are there," Daddy says,

picking her up in his arms and pointing. "See? Can you see?" But Naomi can only see the long, long paper streamers stretching from the people below to the people on the ship. Stephen is hopping about picking up unused rolls on the ground and stuffing them in Daddy's pockets.

"She'll be back soon," Daddy says.

The boat blasts its giant whistle and suddenly all the people's hands are as windy and wild as the branches of the cherry tree and the peach tree in a storm.

"Goodbye!" Stephen shouts. "Goodbye!"

Naomi wishes she could hide inside Mama's coat like she did when she was a baby. She looks down at the white woolly flowers Mama sewed on the bottom of her blue dress. One of them is coming undone. She pulls the wool off for Mama to fix. Mama even put some perfume on the flowers so they would smell real.

When they get home, Naomi puts the wool under her pillow so she can still smell Mama when she goes to bed. Stephen comes to say goodnight.

"Here," he says and gives her three of his streamer

rolls. Naomi will put them in the drawer of Mama's sewing machine for a coming-home present for her.

Daddy says Obasan is going to sleep on a cot in her room until Mama comes back.

In the morning Naomi is surprised to see Obasan's long black hair in a thick braid hanging down her back. Naomi has only seen Obasan's hair in a bun at the back of her head before. Stephen and Naomi watch her as she winds her braid and sticks hairpins in her bun. Hairpins, hairpins—she has a hundred hairpins.

"What has long legs, crooked thighs, no head and no eyes?" Stephen asks.

Obasan does not understand his hairpin riddle. She does not understand English very well. She smiles at Stephen anyway.

Obasan is soft and gentle like Mama. Her velvet dressing gown and her quilt are soft too. Sometimes Naomi curls up in Obasan's cot because her quilt is so fluffy.

Chapter 4

Naomi doesn't understand why Mama is taking so long to come home.

"She'll come back when she can," Daddy says.

Stephen is getting grumpier and grumpier. "But when is that, Daddy?" he asks.

"I don't know exactly," Daddy says.

"You don't know. I don't know. We don't know. They don't know," Stephen says. "Nobody knows anything." Stephen stomps into the music room and plays loud angry music on the piano.

The questions make everyone unhappy. After a while Naomi stops asking. She becomes more and more quiet.

There is a strange new unkindness in the street. One day a big woman wearing a wide hat walks by on the street and says hello to Naomi. Naomi doesn't reply.

"What's the matter?" the woman says crossly, looking down at Naomi. "Cat got your tongue?" Naomi is startled because no adult has ever been cross with her before.

At night Naomi sleeps with her Japanese doll and whispers to her. She wishes and wishes her doll could talk like her picture-book doll that came to life.

"Do you know where Mama is?" Naomi asks the doll. But the doll never speaks.

Naomi pretends that the doll has a teeny tiny voice that only Naomi can hear. When Naomi holds the doll up to Daddy's ear to whisper, Daddy smiles. But he says he can't hear her.

"What's she saying, Button Face?" Daddy asks.

"She's asking you when Mama's coming home," Naomi tells him.

"Oh," Daddy says. Then he stares and stares at the ceiling. "She can't come till the war is over," he says quietly. "We're at war with Japan."

"What's war?" Naomi asks.

Daddy tells her that war is the worst and saddest thing in the world. People get hurt and learn to be afraid. It's like the time the burning match made the fire in Naomi's room. War is more dangerous even than that, Daddy says. It turns friends into enemies. In Canada some people think Japanese Canadians are enemies.

"But we aren't," Daddy says.

One afternoon Stephen comes running home from his music lesson. His glasses are broken. There are black wet crying marks on his face. Obasan is hanging clothes on the line when she sees him. She takes the clothespins out of her mouth and bends down to look at Stephen.

Obasan's voice is *yasashi*, like Mama's. "What happened?" she asks.

Stephen doesn't answer. Obasan takes his broken glasses and they go into the kitchen. She wipes his face.

"What happened?" Naomi whispers.

"You know, Naomi," he says angrily. "You know there's a war."

"Oh," she says, wishing to show that she understands, but she does not.

Stephen goes to school at the David Lloyd

George School. Air raid drills happen these days. A loud, long alarm sounds. *Eeeeeee!* The children stand right away and quickly go out of the classrooms in lines. Outside, they scatter, lying flat on the ground, crouching by hedges or in ditches to hide from bombs.

"Be still," the teachers tell the children, "so the enemy won't see you."

A girl with long ringlets who crouches close to Stephen says to him, "All the Jap kids are going to be sent away and they're bad and you're a Jap." And so, Stephen tells Naomi, is she.

"Are we?" Naomi asks Daddy.

"No," Daddy says. "We're Canadians."

"It's a riddle," Stephen says. "We're both the enemy and not the enemy."

"Why?" Naomi asks.

"Because," Stephen says crossly. Then he picks up his violin. He looks as if he is going to cry.

Naomi takes her doll and goes down to Daddy's study. She knows Stephen doesn't like her to see him cry. Naomi hides under Daddy's cot. She holds her doll tightly.

"Don't cry, Dolly," Naomi says. The doll is crying because Stephen is crying. "There's a war. That's why Stephen got hurt."

The doll jumps up and down angrily on the floor. "War is stupid!" the doll shouts in Naomi's voice. But she can't say words very well. "Toop it! Toop it! Toop it!" she says. The doll is so angry she breaks her pointer finger. Then she cries and cries because she is hurt and wants Mama to come home and fix her.

After a while the doll lies down on her back and stares up at the bottom of the bed. All over the mattress, there are white cotton tufts like bunny tails.

"I wish Mama was here," the doll says. "Then we would be as safe as bunnies."

"Go to sleep, Dolly," Naomi says. "I'll take care of you."

Later at night, Naomi wakes up frightened. The night light in the hall is out. The streetlights are out. Such darkness! This is what Stephen calls a blackout. The whole city is hiding. If an enemy in an airplane sees any lights below, he might drop a bomb. The bomb would make a huge fire and burn the house.

Naomi is so afraid she can hardly move. She

wants to find Daddy. He's playing the piano quietly. She feels her way in the darkness till she finds him.

"Couldn't you sleep, Little One?" he asks.

Naomi climbs into his lap and hugs him tight.

He sings the daffodilly song. And then he sings, "The mountain and the squirrel had a quarrel," a funny song Stephen learned at school. Daddy is trying to make Naomi laugh. But she doesn't feel like laughing now when the whole world is dark.

She understands later what it is about. The darkness is everywhere—in the day as well as the night—in the streetcars, the stores, on the sidewalks. It covers the whole city when all the lights are turned out. It's in the sounds of airplanes. It comes out of the mouths of strangers and even the children who shout, "Jap, Jap. Dirty yellow Jap."

Chapter 5

Daddy is not well. He coughs and coughs. Stephen is not well. His sickness is in the bones of his right leg, which is in a big white cast. It looks like Humpty Dumpty in an eggshell.

These wintry days when Aunt Emily comes to visit, she stands whispering to Daddy and Obasan. Naomi hides behind the big sofa in the living room, but she does not understand what Aunt Emily is saying. She doesn't know that Uncle has been sent far away with hundreds of other men. They are in the mountains and the snow, making roads. Aunt Emily says she can't find his dog.

And Grandma and Grandpa Nakane? They are in huge buildings where cows and horses are kept once a year for the fair. Aunt Emily finds Grandma Nakane sitting like a troll on a bunk bed, her head down. Hundreds and hundreds of other women with children and babies are also here. Grandpa Nakane is in another building. He and Grandma cannot see each other.

"Why not?" the doll asks Naomi.

"Why not?" Naomi asks Stephen.

Stephen doesn't know.

He gives Naomi a crayon to draw on his white cast. Naomi draws cherries with stems on them. "These are for Grandpa Nakane," she says. She draws a big peach. "This is for Grandma Nakane."

Her doll wants to draw a picture too, but she is not good at drawing. "Read me a story then," she says. So Naomi finds one of her favourite picture books. It's about a man called Gulliver, who travels to a country full of tiny people who live in tiny houses. He wears old-fashioned fancy clothes with pointy shoes and a frilly coat, and he has a plumed hat in one hand. His other hand shields his eyes as he gazes out over the sea.

"Wouldn't it be fun," Naomi says, "to find a country full of people so small you could put them in your hand? We could play with them all day and watch them make houses out of pebbles. One cherry would be big enough to feed a whole family."

After looking at the pictures, Naomi goes out to play on the swing. "I wish Grandpa Nakane could be here," she whispers. "I wish Mama could come home. I wish my doll could really talk. I wish you could talk to me, Cherry Tree."

Chapter 6

"You're a big boy, Stephen," Daddy says one day. "You'll be strong again. Take good care of your sister. And Naomi, you take care of Stephen, too." Naomi and Stephen are playing with Stephen's cars and soldiers on the deep blue Indian rug in the living room. The lead soldiers are marching on the zigzag border. They pretend it's a winding road. "Soldiers aren't as much fun as dolls and tea sets," Naomi says. "All they can do is fight and fall down dead."

Daddy is holding the statue of the young man who became Japan's greatest teacher. "Practice your piano, Stephen," Daddy says. "And study by yourself, like Nino-miya Kin-jiro did. Read lots of books." Daddy puts the statue on the floor in front of the toy soldiers and kneels beside Stephen and Naomi. He has to go away, he tells them gently. "Be good children. Study hard. Listen to Obasan. Say your prayers every day."

That's the last thing Daddy says to the children before he goes away. And then one day Obasan says they are going away, too.

"Where are we going?" Stephen asks.

"On a holiday," Obasan says. "Imagine! Mountains! And a train!"

"Are we going for a long time?"

"Perhaps," Obasan says.

"Is Aunt Emily coming too? And Grandpa? And how about Grandma and Grandpa Nakane?"

"No. Just us. It's our holiday," Obasan says.

"We're going on a holiday! We're going on a holiday!" Naomi sings to her doll.

"Hurrah!" says the doll and does a tap dance on the floor.

But on the day they leave, the doll is afraid. She doesn't like the crowding and the noise at the train station. "Don't be scared," Naomi whispers to the doll. The small children are holding their mothers' hands and legs and skirts. Some are holding their own dolls.

None of the children from Naomi's street are here. The children from Stephen's school are not here either. Only lots and lots of Japanese-Canadian children.

The train is full of strangers. It smells of oil and soot and orange peels. When Naomi stands up, she almost falls over, as if she was standing on a rocking chair. The soot on the window ledge jiggles and jumps like little black flies.

A few seats behind them, a young mother with a face like a bird bends over her tiny red-faced baby. The baby's eyes are closed and the mouth is squinched shut, small as a button. If Naomi leans out farther, she can see the tiny pink fist squashed like a marshmallow against the baby's cheek.

"Go and see the new baby," Obasan says. She gives Naomi an orange to take. But Naomi feels shy. There are too many strangers. And Mama and Daddy aren't here.

Obasan finds a towel and some apples and oranges and takes them to the baby's mother. Obasan bumps from side to side as she goes down the aisle. The baby's mother bows deeply. She almost folds herself in half over the baby.

Close to Naomi's seat there's a humpbacked little old woman. Her back is round as a church bell. She bounces off the seat as Obasan comes back. The old woman is so short that when she stands she's shorter than when she was sitting.

"Something for the baby," the old woman says. She begins to take off her white flannel underskirt, holding the train seat with one hand.

"Ah, ah, Grandmother," Obasan says gently.

"It is clean," the old woman says. "Last night it was washed."

Obasan holds her in the rock-rock of the train. They sway together back and forth. The old woman is careful not to let the underskirt touch the floor.

"For a diaper," the old woman says. "She doesn't have anything for the baby." She folds the underskirt into a neat square. Her fingers are stiff and curled. They look like the driftwood you find on the beach.

Obasan bows and takes the present. She puts it on the young mother's lap. Their heads bob like birds as they talk. Naomi holds her doll up so she can watch them.

Outside the train window, the trees are zipping past. What would it be like, Naomi wonders, to be lost in the woods? She would have to walk and walk and walk. But she might never find the way home. At night there might be wolves and bears. Maybe there would even be snakes. What if Naomi climbed up a tree and couldn't get down again?

Far, far away on the side of a mountain, she can see a giant man, higher than the trees, one hand holding a plumed hat against his hip, one hand shielding his eyes. It's Gulliver! She's sure of it. He's dressed in exactly the same costume that he wore in the picture book.

"Look!" she says to Obasan. "Over there. Gulliver!"

Obasan smiles and nods, but she can only see the trees on the mountain. Naomi and her doll can see and hear things that no one else can.

The train goes on and on through tunnels and along the banks of rivers. Naomi brings out her red, white and blue ball, and her Mickey Mouse that can walk by itself down a slope. Naomi asks Stephen if he wants to play, but he stares out the window. He's doing piano exercises with his fingers on his cast.

Naomi puts her doll to bed on a blanket on Obasan's lap. There's enough room for Naomi's head beside the doll. Obasan's face is quiet and calm. Her hand taps Naomi's back as she falls asleep.

"*Nen, nen,*" Obasan sings softly. It's the lullaby Grandma Kato used to sing to Naomi when Naomi was a baby. *Nen, nen, korori...*

Chapter 7

The train coughs and shudders as it stops. What place is this? Out of the window Naomi can see a big lake with a sandy beach and drift logs. The people are all crowding out of the train. Outside, the sudden air is crisp and cool and smells of sawdust. Mountains green with trees climb up to the sky. Across the lake, the highest, farthest mountains are blue and purple and topped with white snow.

Naomi holds onto Obasan's skirt. If she lets go, she's afraid she will be lost. Stephen is hop-hopping on his crutches. So many boxes and bags and pulling and bumping. It's even more crowded than the train station in Vancouver. But there are no streetcars or streetlights here.

"It's Slocan," Stephen says. "Bears are up there," he says, pointing to the mountains, "and eagles and lynxes."

People are bustling about on the wooden plat-form, carrying luggage. A boy in a grey suit has a kit-ten. The kitten's little mouth opens and closes, but there is so much noise Naomi can't hear it mewing.

Stephen is leaning on his crutches. He says, "Hello, Sensei." And there is the round-faced minis-ter from the church in Vancouver. He has round eyes and round glasses, and he is talking to Obasan and a man with a wheelbarrow. And off they all go, walking along a road together—Obasan, Naomi, the minister and the man with the wheelbarrow. Stephen is hop-ping along, sometimes behind, sometimes ahead.

"It is not too far," Sensei says to Obasan. "I will show you the way."

The road winds past houses, then they come to a rickety wooden bridge. Below them the water jumps and skips along, bouncing over the rocks. On the bank of the stream, a crow is hop-hopping on skinny legs as stiff as lead soldiers' legs. Naomi wants her doll to talk to the crow.

"Where's my doll?" Naomi asks, calling to Obasan.

Obasan stops and turns around. She looks at

the luggage on the wheelbarrow. Her voice sounds worried. "*Ara!*" she cries.

She lifts pieces of luggage one by one from the wheelbarrow. The doll is lost.

The man pushing the wheelbarrow says he will find it and squats down in front of Naomi. He slaps his knees as if he has already done it. His round face is full of crinkly laugh lines.

"Did we leave her on the train?" Naomi asks.

"We will ask," the man says.

Naomi wants to cry because her doll is lost. But Obasan says not to worry. She takes a flowery handkerchief out of her purse and says she will show Naomi how to make a doll's hat out of it.

Stephen, even if he is on crutches, is now ahead of everyone. The woods are so thick that Naomi can't see him.

"Wait, Stephen," she calls, running to catch up.

He's staring and staring. "See that?" he says, pointing. Naomi can't see anything except trees and trees and more trees. Beneath them, the ground is soft and bumpy. There are fat pine cones and little acorn hats. Ferns are spread open like green fans.

"Can't you see the house?" Stephen says.

They walk a few more steps and there, hidden in the woods, is a small grey hut.

"That's where we're going to live," Stephen says.

It looks like a giant toadstool. It's surrounded by tall weeds. It doesn't look like a real house, Naomi thinks.

Stephen clumps up the porch steps and pushes open the front door. It scrapes along the floor. How grey everything is. There's a dead bumblebee on the windowsill. Dusty newspapers cover the walls instead of wallpaper. Everything looks grey. Naomi has never seen such a dusty little house.

"See that?" Stephen touches the ceiling with his crutch. "That's grass and manure up there."

"What?"

"Cow manure. That's what they were saying."

The ceiling is so low it reminds Naomi of the house of Snow White and the seven dwarves. Or maybe it's the home of the three bears. But there's no porridge waiting in a great big bowl or a middle-sized bowl or a wee little bowl. There's only the dead bee by the grey window, and the weeds outside that look as if they want to come in.

Chapter 8

Morning comes and the next and the next. When, Naomi wonders, will they go home? And when will she see Mama and Daddy again? Mama, she knows, went to Japan with Grandma Kato. Daddy is in a hospital. Uncle is working somewhere in the woods. And Aunt Emily and Grandpa Kato have gone far away to Toronto. And where are Grandma and Grandpa Nakane?

Today, Obasan and Naomi and Stephen are walking across the bridge. They stop to watch the tiny fish, all swimming together like a grey cloud. It is all so strange. Grandma Nakane, Obasan says, is in heaven now.

"Everyone is born," Obasan says, "and everyone dies someday. If you die when you are old, that is happiness."

"Is Grandma happy?" Naomi asks.

"Yes," Obasan says.

The last time Naomi saw Grandma and Grandpa Nakane, they were on the back of a truck going to a hospital. Obasan held Grandma Nakane's hand. Grandpa Nakane tried to sit up and tried to smile as he waved goodbye to Stephen and Naomi. The ends of his moustache went up and down.

Naomi takes Obasan's hand and they walk down the pebbly road to the hall. The hall is so full that some men and women are standing along the back wall. Some people are holding handkerchiefs to their eyes. Why are they crying? Naomi wonders.

The funeral takes a long time. Obasan gives Naomi a pencil and a small notebook in which to draw. Naomi makes a house with many windows, a triangle roof and triangle windows in the roof—just like her house in Vancouver. She fills the sky with seagulls. She has just learned to make birds like the letter V.

Stephen is sitting on the other side of Obasan. His fingers are digging at a black piece of gum stuck to the bottom of his folding chair. When he gets it off, he leans over Obasan and sticks it on one of Naomi's seagulls.

"Another mosquito for you," he says.

Everyone is praying and the whole hall is full of voices.

Obasan opens her purse for a pen to give to Stephen, but he folds his arms and shakes his head. Naomi takes his gummy mosquito off her picture.

Later at night, Stephen holds a flashlight and leads the way up the steep road to the old silver mine. There is going to be a fire to burn Grandma Nakane's body. Grandpa Nakane wants Grandma Nakane's ashes sent to him.

Obasan is carrying delicious food and cakes for the men to eat.

"Will Grandma be hurt?" Naomi asks.

Obasan shakes her head and smiles. "No," she says.

A full moon is coming out from behind a cloud when they arrive at the clearing near the old mine. An owl calls, *Hoo. Hoo.* A few men are waiting by a high pile of logs. Grandma's coffin rests on top. Obasan bows to the men and puts the food near a pile of wood where it will be seen after they leave. One man pours gasoline from a tin carefully onto the logs. The other lights a cloth on the end of a stick.

What is Grandma thinking? Naomi wonders as she sits on a log beside Obasan.

"*Sa,*" the man carrying the torch says. "Shall we begin?"

He says to Stephen. "Your grandmother and grandfather are my old friends." He hands the stick to Stephen. Stephen hops to the logs, carrying the fire.

Swift as the crack of a whip, the fire shoots along the edge of the log. Before Stephen can reach another corner, all the wood is dancing bright and hot in the night. It's as hot as the sawdust furnace in the basement in Vancouver. Who, Naomi used to think, could live in such heat? The angel in a Bible story was safe in the middle of a fire like that.

"It's in the fire and the heat where the angel is found," Obasan once said. She also said that the best swords are put in the hottest fire, and people too become strong and sharp when life is hardest.

Naomi feels the fire, hot and dry on her face. Obasan has been using a handkerchief to chase the mosquitoes, but now she puts the handkerchief in front of Naomi's face.

Chapter 9

More than anything in the world, Naomi wishes she could go back to be with Mama and Daddy once more in their real house in Vancouver. She doesn't want to live in the house of the three bears with newspaper walls anymore. She wants to sleep in her own room where the picture bird sings above her bed and the real bird sings in the cherry tree in the backyard. But no matter how hard she wishes, they don't go home.

And now, the crowded little grey house is even more crowded. A long-faced woman named Nomura-obasan has come to stay with them. She's not well, Obasan says, and they must take care of her.

"Daddy's sick too," Stephen says. Daddy's letters are from a hospital somewhere in the woods.

"When is he coming here?" Naomi asks. "When will he get better?"

Nobody answers. Nobody knows.

Stephen is playing some music that only he can hear, on a folding cardboard piano Daddy made. *The world is beautiful as long as there is music*, Daddy wrote. *Keep the world beautiful, Stephen. If you listen hard, you can hear all the notes.*

Stephen and Naomi pretend they are at home again in their Vancouver house and the cardboard piano is real. Naomi has to guess which song he is playing. Even if Naomi is older now, she likes the kindergarten songs the best. They remind her of Mama.

One wintry morning, Obasan is washing the breakfast dishes. She fills the basin from the water bucket by the stove. *Plip* says the dipper and *Szt-szt* goes the water as it spills on the hot stove. The box beside the stove is full of logs and kindling. Obasan goes outside into the fluffy falling snow to chop the logs on a stump.

When she comes back in, Obasan says solemnly. "We don't know when Daddy is coming, but Uncle is coming tonight. And there is even more good news. Your cast is going to come off."

"Ah. Good news! Good news!" Nomura-obasan

says, clapping her hands. "Uncle coming. And soon you will run again, Stephen."

"*Sa*," Obasan says brightly. She wipes her hands on her apron. "So much to do."

They are like elves hopping about all afternoon. Obasan soaks dried mushrooms and dried fiddleheads in water. Naomi makes paper decorations and paper baskets for jellybeans. Even Nomura-obasan tries to help, but her hands are too shaky.

As they work, the snow keeps falling. The fence post looks like it's wearing a puffy white hat. Stephen puts his hand on the window to melt the frost so he can see. They wait and wait until it gets dark. Obasan lights the coal-oil lamp with a match, turning up the wick slowly to make it brighter.

At last they hear a *Stomp, stomp* outside. Stephen throws the door open and in comes Uncle in a whoosh of snow.

"Uncle!" Stephen cries.

Uncle puts down his wooden box and sack and shakes the snow off his coat. His arms are as wide as Papa Bear's. "Hello hello," he says as he lifts Stephen up. "What's this?" he asks, poking Stephen's cast.

"It's coming off," Stephen says. "I won't need it anymore."

Obasan takes off her apron. She folds her hands in front. "Welcome home," she says.

Uncle looks at all the food and the decorations on the table. "Ah," he says, "it must be Christmas."

"You have come from so far," Nomura-obasan says. She is sitting up in bed and bows forward. Uncle bows as well, and they both say, "Such a long time."

Then he squats in front of Naomi and scratches his head.

"And this little girl—who can she be?" he asks. He's joking of course. But she wonders if she has changed. Adults are always saying how big the children are getting.

He turns to his sack and takes out two wooden flutes. With a *Whoop*, Stephen leaps to Uncle. And then Stephen's fingers are dancing lightly over the smooth wood. At once the room fills with a bright dancing sound. Uncle slaps his knees as Stephen goes step-hop, step-hop, around and around the wooden box chairs. Stephen is like a rooster, crowing with his head up high. He plays and plays.

"Oh there will be dancing," Nomura-obasan says, tapping her slippers on the floor.

"What a boy!" Uncle says, patting Stephen on the back. "Just like your father."

Chapter 10

With Uncle here now, the house looks tidier with new shelves and narrow benches. Outside there are neat stacks of chopped wood in a shed. Uncle is very busy. In the spring he makes a garden and plants carrot seeds and snow peas and long white radishes and spinach.

When he's not working, Uncle takes the children on hikes up the mountain. Up and up they go. Naomi thinks if they climb all the way, they will reach the sky. Stephen's cast is off, but he still does not run very well. When he is tired, he leans to the side and even though he is going slowly, he looks as if he's in a hurry.

"It will take time," Obasan says. "Life is not easy."

In the early spring, curly fiddleheads poke out of the ground like green question marks. *Snip!* And into the jam pails they go. But into the mouths pop the tart red strawberries the size of shirt buttons. Later there are gooseberries, shiny and green and round as marbles. Uncle examines floppy dark mushrooms on dead trees and other plump ones hiding in the soft mossy earth because he's the only one who knows which are safe to eat.

From a high rocky ledge past a waterfall, they look down at the world. Far below are the little houses and the silvery river shimmering on its way to the lake. And farther away to the left, there are rows and rows of tiny toy-block houses with pencil-thin lines of smoke curling out of chimneys.

"Two families in one small house. One room for one family. We are lucky," Uncle says, shaking his head.

One summer day, Obasan is washing clothes, Uncle is chopping wood, Stephen is writing a letter to Daddy and Naomi is at the lake. She is with Kenji, a boy her age who lives in one of the tiny houses. His wobbly glasses bounce up and down his nose when he jumps.

Kenji is paddling around on a log raft. Naomi

would like to go with him but Uncle says she must not go on rafts. The water is cool and tickly against her toes.

She is wearing her green and white knit bathing suit. Close by is the sandcastle village. They are making sand houses with grass-top trees and white-pebble sidewalks. There are twig chimneys, twig bridges, twig people and one fat twig dog with three legs.

Kenji and Naomi are playing when Rough Lock Bill comes to watch. Rough Lock Bill is a tall skinny man with hair like seaweed. He sits on the sand and talks to the children as they play. Naomi can see his big toe sticking out of his sock.

"What's your name?" he asks Naomi.

"Naomi," Kenji replies.

"Can't talk, eh?" He nods and hands her a stick. "Here," he says, "Can you print? Print your name."

Naomi brushes the wet sand off her hands and takes the stick. NAOMI, she prints in large letters.

"Aha," Rough Lock Bill says. "Naomi."

He picks up one of the stick people. "Is this you?" he asks Naomi.

She shakes her head. He picks up all the stick

people and tells stories. When he gets tired he goes back to his house beside the beach. Naomi can see him rocking in his chair.

Kenji gets tired of the sand village. "Let's go in the water," he says. He jumps up and runs to his raft. The raft wobbles as he gets on.

"Come on, Naomi!" he calls. A long pole is in his hand. He pushes the raft closer to the shore. "Climb on," he says. "I won't go far."

The water makes her toes curl up tight. She has never gone into deep water, but she kneels on the wobbly raft.

"Okay," Kenji says. He leans on the pole. The raft scoots out over the water. She lies down on the wet logs. Her toes dangle over the edge. There are small grey fish swimming beside them. The water feels colder the deeper it gets. When Naomi looks up, she can't see the sand village at all.

"It's too far here, Kenji," she says. "Let's go back."

"Just one more shove," Kenji says. He leans back, lifting one leg and the pole high in the air. Down goes the pole straight into the water. Then—*Splash!* Kenji tumbles sideways and falls overboard. *Whoosh!* The cold water sprays over Naomi's back, and the raft bounces on the waves. She feels like a cat on a see-saw. There's nowhere to hold. She's on her hands and knees, trying to balance.

Kenji is paddling around and shaking the water out of his hair. He has his glasses in his teeth, like a dog. She can see the pole bobbing away behind her, out of reach. Kenji's trying to say something through his teeth as he swims to shore. But Naomi can't hear him.

When he gets near the beach he stands up and waves to her.

"Jump!" he shouts.

"I can't!" she shouts back. "I can't swim!"

He holds his hands up to the sides of his head. He can't see without his glasses. Then slowly, he steps backwards till he's out of the water.

Naomi knows he can't help her. He doesn't know how to help. He's afraid. He turns and runs down the beach. He won't come back.

The raft drifts in the still lake. Last month a boy drowned in this lake. She must decide quickly what to do. If she waits, the raft will go farther and farther and she'll be lost.

She feels sick and afraid. Then she jumps.

Down she goes. Down, down, down. Water is in her ears. Water is in her nose. Water is in her head. Water is everywhere. She can't breathe. She can't see. She can't tell where the air is or where the shore is. She splashes and gasps, and swallows air and water. Again and again she's whirled in the choking dizziness. She tries to cry out, but the sound she makes is like an animal growling.

After a horrible time, something is pulling her along through the water. She feels as limp as laundry on a line. Suddenly her ears clear. There's a *Whack, Whack* on her back.

"Okay, okay, I gotcha," a man's voice says.

Water gushes from her nose and mouth. Between gasps, she is breathing. She is breathing and she knows she is safe.

Rough Lock Bill places her on her stomach on the sand. He turns her head sideways on his red and blue-checkered shirt. She can feel the sand against her cheek. When she moves her knees up, more water comes out of her stomach and nose and throat. She wipes her nose on the sleeve and closes her eyes.

"That's it," Rough Lock says. He peers at her. "Good kid."

After a while, Rough Lock Bill carries her piggyback back to her family. He tells Stephen what happened, and Stephen tells Obasan and Uncle.

"Thank you. Thank you," Uncle says to Rough Lock Bill. "Thank you for saving Naomi."

Chapter 11

Naomi and Obasan are in the bathhouse in Slocan with lots of women and children, all naked and happy together. Uncle and Stephen are on the other side of the wall in the men's bathhouse.

The clothes are piled neatly on a long shelf above the bench along the wall. On the wood-slatted floor in front of the big steamy bath, Naomi squats, scrubbing Obasan's back hard with her washcloth rolled tight. *Rub, rub, rub.* Little rolls of skin come off as if she were erasing Obasan's back. Next comes the slushy soapy washcloth.

Nomura-obasan is here too, washing her hair. She's well enough now and is going to move back to her daughter's family.

Naomi dips the square wooden basin into the big square bath full of steamy hot water. It's just as hot as the baths she used to take with Grandma

Kato. *Swish!* And over Obasan's back and Nomura-obasan's head pours the hot, hot water. So many girls and women are soaking and chatting in the lazy foggy room. When Naomi rinses all the soap off, they climb back in with the others. Naomi feels so drowsy she almost falls asleep.

Nomura-obasan says her daughter is going to be teaching at the new kindergarten that Uncle helped to build. The school and the kindergarten are in the same place as the rows and rows of tiny houses.

The winding path to the school is through the forest. Naomi takes her lunch of salty plum *onigiri*, fiddlehead greens and boiled egg in a light metal lunchbox with a diagonal slot in the lid for chopsticks. Stephen's sandwich and apple are in a paper bag.

On the way home, Stephen and Naomi walk by a big white house. There's a swing in the backyard. A pretty girl about Naomi's age lives there. She has light golden hair like Goldilocks, and her eyebrows are light coloured too. Sometimes before they reach her yard, they can see her swinging. Higher and higher she goes, her toes pointing up to the sky.

One day they stand at the fence and watch her.

"Boy," Stephen says. "I bet she'll go right around."

Toys are all over her backyard. There's a doll carriage, a dollhouse, and a doll's tea set on a doll's table. It makes Naomi think of the dolls and tea sets that she left in her house in Vancouver. And there are two real live white bunnies hopping in a pen. "Oh, I wish I could hold them," Naomi says. They look as fluffy and soft as cotton wool.

The golden-haired girl sees Naomi and Stephen standing at the fence. She scrapes her feet on the ground to stop her swinging. Then she jumps off.

"What are you staring at?" she asks. She sounds angry. Naomi wants to run away into the trees.

The girl makes a face and stomps her feet. "Go away!" she shouts.

What a mean girl, Naomi thinks. "Come on," she says to Stephen. She starts to walk down the path.

But Stephen is angry. He whacks at the grass with his lunch pail.

"Go 'way!" the girl shouts again.

"Why should I?" Stephen says. "This is a free country."

"It's not your country," the girl says.

"It is so!" Stephen shouts back.

"It is not!"

A red-and-white checkered curtain in the window behind the girl moves. There's a woman, who also has golden hair, looking out at Naomi and Stephen. She raps on the window with her knuckles. The girl looks back. The woman is shaking her head.

"I can't play with you," the girl says in a singsong voice. She points her chin to the sky and turns her head.

Naomi runs through the trees, taking a shortcut away from the path. The thick pine-needle floor crackles as Naomi goes. She can hear Stephen behind her, hitting the trees with his lunch pail.

Chapter 12

Naomi doesn't like the horrid girl. She doesn't like walking by the horrid girl's house. She doesn't like going to school either. In the morning Obasan combs Naomi's long hair and braids it in thick pigtails. Naomi doesn't like her pigtails.

But she likes to climb the mountains. She likes playing with her Mickey Mouse who can walk by itself down a slope. She likes reading her school reader. And she likes reading the comics in the newspaper.

There are some funny roly-poly comic strip boys called the Katzenjammer Kids. They play tricks on a naughty little rich boy called Rollo. And there's a fuzzy-haired girl with empty circle eyes, called Little Orphan Annie, who is always saved from danger by her Daddy Warbucks. Sometimes Naomi lies in her bunk bed at night pretending that she is Little Orphan Annie being rescued by her daddy.

Stephen likes to read the comics too. But he also reads the harder parts of the newspaper. He says he has to know what's happening in the war. Uncle and Stephen talk about the war together while they chop wood.

At school they all sing "O Canada" and "God save the King," and they salute the flag. On Saturday nights, the children sometimes go to see the movies and the news at the Odd Fellows Hall. When they watch war movies, they feel afraid of the terrible enemies who are more horrible than anyone can imagine.

One day Stephen comes running home with a red, white and blue flag. It's called the Union Jack, the same as the flag high up on the pole at school. The flag flaps behind him as he runs round and round.

"Where did you get that?" Naomi asks.

"I won it," Stephen says. "I traded all my marbles for it." Back and forth he waves the flag. Then he nails it to a long pole and plants it in a hole at the top of Uncle's rock garden. The flag hangs quietly and peacefully high up in the air.

When Stephen jumps back down again, he stands at attention, facing the flag. Then he salutes it, saying, "God save the King." He makes a trumpet out of his hands and they sing "Land of Hope and Glory" and "O Canada." When they are singing "Hearts of Oak," Naomi sees the horrid girl walking up the path.

They stop. She stops too. She's staring at them and staring at the flag.

"That's not your flag," she says.

"It is too," Stephen says.

"You stole it!" she shouts. "Give it to me!"

"It's mine!" Stephen shouts back.

"You're going to lose the war," she says in her singsong voice.

"We will NOT!" Stephen yells so loudly that Naomi covers her ears and runs into the house.

From inside the house Obasan and Naomi listen to Stephen pounding on the tub drum. Obasan is calmly making supper.

Stephen stops drumming and comes into the house. He lies down on his bunk bed and takes the flute from under his pillow. All the songs he can remember, he plays and plays and plays. Even when it's time to sleep he keeps playing. Uncle joins in with the *tappity-tappity* sounds of spoons on his knees.

"Good music," Uncle says to Stephen.

"Good drumming, Uncle," Stephen replies.

"I bet you think music is the best thing," Naomi says.

"No," Stephen says. "The best thing is to be free. If we were free, we could go home."

"Ah. When you play music, you are free," Uncle says.

Chapter 13

It's around noon. Naomi and Stephen are playing at the side of the house, making a little pond with a bowl of water, rocks and flowers. Obasan is knitting. All Naomi's clothes from Vancouver are too small now and Obasan is adding longer sleeves to make her sweater bigger.

Naomi is putting a buttercup in the bowl for a pretend lily pad when she hears someone calling, "Hi!"

The horrid girl and her mother are in the middle of the road. They are both shielding their eyes from the sun as they look up. The flag flaps coolly in the mountain air.

"Hello," the mother says. "I heard your flute. And I heard you both singing our national anthem last night when I was out for a walk. My, but you have a lovely voice, young man. And you are a fine, fine player.

Oh yes, you are indeed. Indeed you are."

Stephen stands up and puts his feet apart, his hands on his hips. He is scowling at the horrid girl, who is standing with her arms folded and pouting. He marches to the foot of the flag and stands at attention in front of it.

"This is my flag," Stephen says. "This is my country. I don't care what you say."

"Yes," the mother says, nodding her head sadly. "Of course it is your flag. And it is our flag too. We have come over to say we are sorry for being unkind, haven't we, Mitzi?"

The horrid girl is looking down at her shoes. She kicks the grass and shakes her head. Then she comes over to Naomi and leans her head to the side. "My name is Mitzi," she says. "What's your name?"

"Naomi."

"Hello, Naomi," Mitzi's mother says. "And what is your brother's name?"

"Stephen."

"Tell Stephen you're sorry for being unkind," Mitzi's mother says.

Mitzi makes a face at her mother and tosses her

head. "I don't like boys," she says and turns around and stomps. Then she comes over to Naomi and puts her hand to Naomi's ear. "Can you come and play at my house?" she whispers.

Naomi can hardly believe what she is hearing. Will Mitzi let her play with her fluffy white rabbits?

"Ask your mother," Mitzi says.

Mitzi doesn't know that Obasan is not Naomi's mother.

Naomi runs inside to ask. Obasan puts down her knitting and nods gently, giving Naomi a bag of cookies.

"For Mitzi," Obasan tells Naomi and goes outside with her.

"Oh, thank you," Mitzi's mother says when Naomi gives them to Mitzi. "Say 'Thank you,' Mitzi."

"Can I eat one?" Mitzi asks.

Obasan smiles and Mitzi's mother smiles. It seems to Naomi that the trees and the birds and the sun and the flag and all the creatures in the whole world are smiling right now.

Mitzi skips down the path, munching the cookie.

"Come on!" she calls to Naomi. Naomi feels too

shy to skip but she walks quickly to keep up.

When they come to her yard, Mitzi breaks one cookie into little pieces. She puts them in a little doll's dish on her doll's table.

All afternoon they play together. Naomi cuddles Mitzi's bunnies. At first they make little jerky jumping movements with their back feet. But afterwards they get used to Naomi. They eat sticks of carrots and pieces of lettuce. Their wriggly noses sniff and sniff. One is called Patsy and the other is called Gruff. Mitzi tells Naomi that when they have babies Naomi can have one. Naomi wants to jump up and run home and tell Stephen.

Almost every day after this, Mitzi and Naomi play. They make up games and concerts. They make a playhouse out of blankets in the trees. They make mud pies and pine-needle tea and have tea parties with the dolls. They make secret codes. One time they find a dead bird and bury it, wrapped in birchbark, in the woods. They promise they will be friends to birds forever. And they print a secret on the birchbark and put it under the stone that marks the mossy place where the bird is buried. Another time, when they are playing house, Mitzi wears Naomi's blue bead necklace. Mitzi likes it so much Naomi lets her keep it.

Mitzi has three favourite dolls. One has eyes that close with a *click* sound when she is laid on her back. She's a fancy doll in a lacy pink dress and white socks, white shoes and tiny white shoelaces. When she is spanked or put on her stomach, she makes a crying noise.

The second doll is a Raggedy Ann with long pigtails like Naomi has. She was a Christmas present when Mitzi was four. Mitzi loves her Raggedy Ann the best.

"I want braids like yours and my dolly's," Mitzi says.

"I want curly golden hair like yours," Naomi tells Mitzi.

"Let's trade," Mitzi says. They giggle because they know they can't do that.

Mitzi's third favourite doll is the most dear baby doll that Naomi has ever seen. It has big blue eyes and chubby little arms and legs. She drinks from a bottle and wets her diaper. Her name is Baby.

When they get tired of playing with Mitzi's

dolls, they play hide-and-go-seek and Mother-may-I, and they skip with one end of her skipping rope tied to a tree. They read Mitzi's storybooks and play with paper dolls and jacks and colour in colouring books and make shadow plays with a sheet. They swing and eat tea biscuits that are just like the ones Mama used to make. Most of all Naomi likes making up adventure stories about Mitzi and herself. She pretends they are magic and can become invisible or tiny as Tom Thumb or Momotaro in the peach. Sometimes the giant Gulliver comes and carries them away to be with elves and fairies in the forest.

On Naomi's birthday, Mitzi brings her a present in a box so big she can barely carry it.

"What is it?" Naomi asks.

The box is wrapped in white tissue paper and has a big pink bow.

"Guess," Mitzi says.

It's not a heavy box. Naomi holds it and rattles it and shakes it. It doesn't make a sound.

"I can't guess," she tells Mitzi. What could be so light and in such a big box?

Naomi unties the bow carefully and opens the

box. All she can see are big handfuls of crumpled tissue paper. She wonders if it's a joke and Mitzi has brought an empty box.

"Keep going," Mitzi says as Naomi takes out the paper.

Naomi takes out more crumples. And then… and then…Naomi sees her. It's Baby! It's the dearest, sweetest doll that there ever was. Naomi is too surprised for words. She puts her hands down into the crumples and lifts Baby up gently. She's wearing a brand new pink knitted dress with little pink booties and a pink and white bonnet. Her bottle is around her wrist with an elastic band.

"Oh!" Naomi holds her in her arms.

"Isn't she pretty?" Mitzi says. "Mommy made the dress."

Naomi hardly dares to ask if she can keep her.

"It's your birthday present," Mitzi says.

Naomi wants to laugh and cry at the same time. She must be the luckiest, happiest girl alive. She wraps a tea towel around Baby and cradles her in her arms.

"Can I really, really keep her?" she asks.

"Yes," Mitzi says.

Chapter 14

Early one morning, Naomi wakens while it's still dark outside. Obasan and Uncle are awake. Stephen is sleeping in the bunk below. His mouth is squished open on his pillow.

A few days ago, Stephen came running home, shouting that the war was over. "We won we won we won!" he cried. He ran behind the house with both hands high in the air. His fingers were raised in the V-for-Victory sign. He pulled the flag out of the rock garden. Then up he climbed onto the shed and still higher to the roof of the house. The flag was up as high as it could go.

This morning there's no shouting. A log drops, *Thud*, as it burns in the wood stove. The coal-oil lamp is on. Beside the lamp, Baby is sitting on a tin of sardines. She's looking out the window.

Last week, Mitzi and Raggedy Ann and Baby and

Naomi had a tea party in the playhouse. A chipmunk came to visit. It was the first time Baby had seen a chipmunk up close. Baby threw a temper tantrum when the chipmunk went away. She's getting quite spoiled, Naomi thinks. After the doll came home, she wanted to sit on the table every night to watch for chipmunks.

"Stephen," Naomi whispers, leaning over the side of the bunk. She blows into his face. "Wake up," she says. Stephen keeps sleeping.

"So early?" Uncle whispers as Naomi takes Baby off the sardine tin.

"Not sleepy?" Obasan also whispers. Her long braid is dangling down her back. She is at the stove, quietly putting in a piece of wood. She puts her finger to her mouth, and hands Naomi a slice of bread that is toasting on the stove.

Naomi gives a corner to Baby and another one for her to give to the chipmunk. Outside a dog is barking. A light wind is blowing through the branches of the trees.

While Naomi finishes the toast, she notices that the other room has been changed around and there are piles of boxes everywhere. Nomura-obasan went away months ago to stay with her daughter. But her cot is in the room again. Has she come back?

"Who's here?" Naomi asks, standing on tiptoe.

The sleeping person is facing the other way and an arm covers the head. The arm moves then. Naomi can see the back of the head, the straight black hair just like Daddy's.

Is it Daddy? Can it be Daddy? Naomi's hands drop with a slap to her thighs. It is! It is!

Without turning his head, he lifts his finger and beckons.

"Good morning, my Naomi," he says.

How does he know it's her? She hasn't made a sound.

He turns then and smiles. It's her very own father—her Daddy who plays the violin and sings, her Daddy who rocks her in the rocking chair, her Daddy who nibbles her tea biscuits and stands on a ladder to pick the cherries and the ripest peaches.

Naomi jumps over a box onto the cot and she is in his arms again—her father's arms.

His hands touch her face. She wraps her arms around his neck. The button of his pyjama top presses

into her cheek. She can feel his heart's steady thump, thump, thump.

They are as quiet as moon song. As quiet and still as resting swans. Into this quiet she falls like a feather floating.

They do not talk. Only Uncle says "Ah," as he swallows his tea. Obasan's butter knife makes a scrape-scrape noise on the toast. And the neighbour's dog outside barks excitedly.

Then suddenly Stephen is in the room. He stands there barefoot, rubbing the sleep from his eyes. His flute is in his hand.

"Good morning, my man," Daddy says.

"Dad!" Stephen jumps on them and howls. Daddy holds both his children in his arms. They rock and sway together on the little cot.

Then Stephen gets Daddy the other flute, and they play and play until the sky grows light.

"Whoo," Daddy says finally. "Not bad, my son."

"Not bad," Uncle says.

Obasan turns down the coal-oil lamp. She cups her hand behind the chimney and blows out the night light. Then she gives them all pieces of toast.

Chapter 15

After breakfast, Daddy and Uncle talk quietly. Naomi doesn't understand what they are saying, but Daddy looks sad.

"We're moving," Stephen says.

"Moving? Are we going home?"

"No."

"Why not?"

"We can't."

"Why not?"

Stephen says that everyone is going away again. But he doesn't know where.

Naomi packs her Mickey Mouse and the red, white and blue ball in a crumple of newspapers. She is not going to pack Baby. She will carry her. Stephen wraps his flute carefully in the sleeve of his sweater. He gives the other flute to Daddy.

"Are you coming with us, Daddy?" Naomi asks.

He's working more slowly and looks tired as he puts his fingers on the holes of the flute.

"No, my Button," Daddy says. "I can't. But God's angels are going with you."

"Why can't you come with us?" Naomi asks.

Obasan hands her a dish. She asks her to wrap it in newspaper. Naomi knows that Obasan doesn't want her to ask questions right now. And she knows Daddy has to go back to a hospital. But she wants to be near him. She wants him to come with them.

"It's not fair," she whispers. She wants to run away with him. But there's nowhere to go.

When it gets dark, they can hear music wavering through the trees. A loudspeaker is playing "Auld Lang Syne." While they are packing, they hear voices and footsteps. Some people are coming towards the house.

"Good evening," a familiar voice calls.

Obasan opens the door and Nomura-obasan comes in, bowing deeply.

"Such a busy time," she says. She's thinner than before and holds a cane. With her is an old man wearing a suit.

"Good evening," the old man says. His voice sounds as scratchy as the screen door.

"Ah, ah," Nomura-obasan says when she sees Daddy. There are tears in her eyes. "Such a long time. A long long time."

"Such a long time," the old man also says. He puts his shaking hand on Daddy's shoulder.

Obasan pushes the boxes aside as the round-faced minister comes in next. He takes a long black gown and a shorter white gown out of his black bag.

"Let us pray," Sensei says as people kneel on the floor. "This is the last supper."

The old man tries to kneel but he can't. He leans on his stick.

Naomi's eyes are supposed to be closed. But she's peeking at everyone's feet. The minister's boots rock back and forth as everyone recites the prayers. The Japanese words spoken quickly sound like the rustling leaves in the fall when the wind blows them about.

The old man's false teeth make a clacking sound. His voice wheezes as he stumbles to keep up to the others. Nomura-obasan can't keep up either. She's shaking so much that Obasan has to hold her.

When the service is finished, the minister starts to sing a goodbye song, his voice strong and deep. He flings his head back.

Till we meet
Till we meet
God be with us
Till we meet again.

Daddy's eyes are closed. He's trying to sing too, but his rich baritone voice is weak. Sometimes he stops. The old man's singing is out of tune with the others, and he takes breaths in between, sitting down finally on a wooden box as the others continue.

Mata o – o – o
Hima de –e

It is as if the old man is singing alone to his own rhythm. As everyone else stops singing, he continues, his voice straining. "Once more," the minister says. "Let us sing."

The voices fill the tiny room and Naomi takes in the sound as if the music could shut out the darkness.

When the song ends for the third time, Obasan

takes the old man's bony hands in her own. "We will meet again some day," she says.

Nomura-obasan draws a handkerchief from her sleeve and holds it over her face. The minister puts his hand on her back and says, "In a time like this, let us trust in God even more. To trust when life is easy is no trust."

"There is a time for crying," the old man says in his wavery voice. "Someday the time for laughter will come."

"Yes, that must be so," the minister says. "We will meet again."

He puts a hand on Stephen's head. "Be a great musician like your father," he says. Next he turns to Naomi. "Be sturdy." He bows to everyone—long, low bows. Then he is gone, trotting rapidly down the path to the next waiting group.

Chapter 16

Daddy goes back to the hospital the next day. And after a few more days, the time comes for Stephen and Naomi and Uncle and Obasan to leave.

"We have to say goodbye to Mitzi now," Naomi tells Baby.

Obasan and Naomi take a cake with them. When Obasan visits anyone, she always takes a present.

"Goodbye, Baby," Mitzi says, kissing her old doll.

"Goodbye, Raggedy Ann," Naomi says.

Naomi says goodbye to all the dolls and the bunnies, Patsy and Gruff. There are new little baby bunnies and she says goodbye to each one. She says goodbye to the swing and the playhouse. They start giggling as she says goodbye to the tea set and the table and the doll dresses and the colouring books and the chipmunk who isn't even there.

"God bless you all," Mitzi's mother says as they leave.

At the train station there are boxes and luggage and hundreds and hundreds of people. It's like the day when they first came to Slocan. The black noisy train clangs its bell and hisses back and forth.

Some of the children Naomi used to meet at the bath and at school are here. Above the noisy crowd, the scratchy loudspeaker plays "Auld Lang Syne." Kenji's older brother is in front of Stephen with a black bag over his shoulder. Naomi can't see Kenji.

Hoo—oot! goes the train. One by one, they move along like a giant caterpillar. Uncle is behind Naomi and lifts her up onto the steps.

Inside the train, it's just like the time when they left Vancouver so long ago, except that Uncle is with them and Stephen doesn't have a big cast on his leg. They sit in two seats facing each other. Kenji's brother is ahead and there are some other people Naomi knows. The minister and his family are on this train too.

People outside are waving and waving. Some are crying. It's sad to say goodbye. Naomi is remembering the time at the boat in Vancouver when Mama went away. She wonders where Mama is now. And where, she wonders, is her old doll.

The train shudders and starts to move. Naomi presses her face against the window. Stephen and Uncle stand up to wave as they pull away from the station. Then almost right away, they move into the thick trees and can no longer see anyone.

It's goodbye to the mountains, the lake, to Rough Lock Bill, the school, the bathhouse. "Goodbye, everything. Goodbye, everyone," Naomi whispers, her nose against the train window. They enter a high tunnel as they race along—*Clackity-clack, clackity-clack, clackity-clack.* "So long, Slocan."

Chapter 17

They ride through the shadowy mountain forests, past waterfalls, along skinny high ledges above canyons and out at last into the wide prairie. The flat, brown earth stretches on and on. Naomi falls asleep on the train and when she wakes up they are on the back of a farmer's truck, she and Stephen and Uncle and Obasan, riding down a bumpy gravel road in Alberta. *Bumpitty bump. Rumble rumble.* A tunnel of dust plumes behind them.

The air here is angry and hits out suddenly like a wild man. It blows dust and dirt into Naomi's face. She turns around and turns around and squeezes her eyes shut, but she can't get away. Dried bunches of scratchy weeds tumble along and get stuck on the miles and miles of barbed-wire fences.

Their hut is even smaller than the one in Slocan. There's just one room. Out of one window they can see the huge farm machines that look like skeletons of dinosaurs. Obasan puts rags and newspapers around the bottom of the door and the windows. She's trying to keep out the dust and the flies. But they keep coming in anyway. In summer the windows are covered with a mesh of flies. They walk on Naomi's arms with their sticky hairy feet. They walk on her head and land in her food. Ugh!

There is no bathhouse here. Their bath is a round tub. Getting water is such hard work, especially in winter. Naomi puts on her boots and coat and out she goes with the buckets. The hole gets frozen over and Uncle has to chop it open with a long-handled axe. Naomi can hardly lift the heavy pails. The water sometimes spills down her boots, and her feet get itchy and red.

After everyone takes baths, Obasan washes the clothes in the same water. Naomi helps Obasan hang them outside in the icy wind where they get stiff as cardboard. It's so cold her face stings and her eyelids freeze.

Naomi hates it here. She hates it so much that she wants to run away. So does Stephen.

"Why can't we go back?" she asks Uncle. "Even

if we can't go home to Vancouver, can't we go back to Slocan?"

"Someday. Maybe someday," Uncle says. But someday never comes.

In the spring, they have to work, work, work. The field stretches on forever and is full of rows of plants. All day long they hoe the weeds. It gets so hot it feels like an oven, and Naomi thinks they are gingerbread cookies baking to bits.

Sometimes Naomi gets sick from the heat and lies down in the dirt. Then Uncle comes running across the field. He carries her to the root cellar or to the ditch water. The root cellar is cool, but the rotten potatoes smell horrible. She would rather sit under the bridge in the muddy brown water even if the thistles on the ditch bank sting her feet.

The school in Granton is different from the one in Slocan. Most of the children are not Japanese Canadians like Stephen and Naomi. And the other children don't have to stay at home to work in the fields. The teachers send Naomi and Stephen their homework to do at night.

In harvest time, Obasan wraps rags around Naomi's wrists. She says it helps to lift the heavy beets. But Naomi doesn't like the rags. She doesn't like to look dirty and ragged and ugly in the dusty field. She has to wear Stephen's old clothes. None of her dresses and skirts fit anymore, and she doesn't have pretty clothes. For school, Obasan fixes her old dresses to fit Naomi. But they don't fit properly. Obasan says they are beautiful silks. But Naomi hates them. She wants store-bought dresses like the white girls have.

Naomi writes long letters to Daddy in the hospital. *Now that the war is over, is Mama coming back?* she asks Daddy. *And when can you come?*

He can't come to be with them, Stephen says, until the doctor says he can work. And no one knows where Mama and Grandma Kato are in Japan. Uncle says Aunt Emily is trying to find out.

Daddy always sends music to Stephen. Stephen saves the sheets of music and ties them all together with shoelaces. One evening he's finally finished helping Uncle with the irrigating job, digging ditches. He takes out all of Daddy's music and kneels to get the flute from under the bunk bed.

"Uncle!" Stephen cries out. He holds the flute up for Uncle to see. There is a long crack all the way down the side.

"Ah, the air is too dry," Uncle says sadly.

Stephen and Uncle try tying it together and taping it. But when Stephen plays it, there is only the sound of wind. He tries and tries until Uncle says finally, "It can't be helped."

Stephen takes Daddy's music and a flashlight and runs out of the house. They can hear him getting on the old CCM bike that Uncle bought for him from the farmer.

Obasan stands at the door, but Stephen doesn't turn around to wave goodbye or to say where he is going. From the window they can see the light from his flashlight bouncing up and down as he goes down the road.

Bedtime passes and still Stephen doesn't come home. He doesn't come home all night long. Early the next morning, as Uncle is getting ready to go look for him, they can see Stephen riding his bike. He looks like a dot on the road.

Obasan has been sitting up most of the night.

She has left the coal-oil lamp on in the window. "Where did you go?" Obasan asks.

Stephen just shrugs his shoulders. He doesn't want to talk.

Uncle doesn't say anything.

The next day when they are hoeing, Stephen tells Naomi he went to the United Church in Granton. A window was open. He climbed in and felt around till he found the piano. He also found a blanket and covered the piano so it would be quieter. He was afraid he might get caught. Then he played Daddy's music until the flashlight batteries died.

"Want to hear Daddy's songs?" he asks. The tunes he whistles are so happy they make Naomi want to dance.

Stephen says that when the flashlight went dead, he took the blanket off the piano and fell asleep.

"When I grow up," Stephen says, "I'm going to have a piano and a violin and another flute. I really am, Naomi. And a trumpet too."

"I believe you, Stephen," Naomi says as she whacks out the weeds.

Chapter 18

Across the field from Naomi's hut is a swampy slough with bulrushes, where the cows stand about, mooing and chewing. Naomi comes here and sits under a dead tree, reading and studying by herself like Nino-miya Kin-jiro. What a lot of creatures there are in the slough! The more she stares, the more she sees—wriggly tadpoles, dragonflies, water spiders, mosquito twisters, jelly eggs.

Sometimes Naomi pretends she's back in the mountains. But it isn't like the mountains at all.

One Saturday after supper, she is at the swamp again. *Croak breep, Croak breep.* The frogs and toads are busy arguing. A meadowlark sings. All along the edge of the land, the sky is on fire. Mama said that a match was safe if you could blow it out. But what if the whole world was on fire?

Down the long prairie road, three people are

walking towards Naomi. It's as if they are in a fierce red and purple gigantic furnace.

The Bible tells a story of an angel and three men in a fiery furnace. Who are these three? And where is their angel? Naomi wonders. Daddy said that God's angels would be with her. Maybe the whole burning sky is full of angels.

Closer and closer they come. Aha! It's Stephen pushing his bike and Uncle carrying a bucket. Obasan is in the middle.

Naomi stands up to wave. "Hi!"

Plip, ploop—the frogs and toads dive into the water and the swamp sounds vanish. Uncle and Obasan wave back. Stephen is whistling. He's trying to copy the meadowlark. Naomi thinks Stephen's angel must fly through the air, gathering music.

"Hello, hello," Uncle calls.

"Coming with us?" Stephen asks.

"Some big mushrooms in the ditch over there," Uncle says, pointing.

They walk along till they come to a sandy stretch. Thorny pink rose bushes grow on the other side of the ditch. And there, along the whole stretch of sand in front of the wild roses, is a big crop of plump mushrooms.

"Such treasures," Uncle says, as he fills his pail.

Stephen cuts off a rose with his jackknife and puts it on top of the mushrooms. There are still lots left to pick.

On the way home, Obasan brings an envelope out of her pocket. "A letter for you, Naomi."

"Oh!" Naomi is surprised.

"Open it," Stephen says. "Come on, open it."

She recognises the handwriting, and she can feel something stiff, a white piece of cardboard inside. She reads the letter first. It isn't very long. It goes like this:

Dear Naomi,

I am fine. How are you? It is raining today. If you get this please write to me right away.

Goodbye,

Your best pal,

Mitzi

P.S. Remember the secret? Don't tell anyone. Send me a card like mine.

Super P.S. My mother says to say hello to everyone.

Extra Super P.S. How is Baby? Smudge the chipmunk says to say hello.

Extra extra etc. etc. There are more baby bunnies. I wish you could have one.

That's the end of the letter. Naomi can guess what's on the cardboard. I'll bet anything I'm right, she thinks, but I won't look yet. She reads the letter again and giggles, thinking about Smudge saying hello.

"Who wrote?" Stephen asks.

Naomi shows him the letter. But she won't show anyone what's on the cardboard.

By the time they get back to the hut, the air is cool and a few stars are in the sky. Naomi climbs to the top bunk where she can be alone and hides under the blanket with a flashlight.

She was right! There's a small blotchy mark on the card beside her name. *This is blood* it says under the mark. Above the mark is a verse:

We two are a sisterhood.
We seal this secret
With our blood.

"Blood sisters!" Naomi feels like jumping out of

the covers. But she must not let anyone know. It's a secret. A blood sister is forever. If she tells anyone, the magic will be broken and the secret will be destroyed. The power is in the secret. If one of them gets caught in a war, she has the power to rescue the other.

They talked about it when they found the dead bird in the woods. "Maybe we can make the bird come back to life," Mitzi said.

"You mean if we're blood sisters?" Naomi asked.

"Yes. But we need blood to be blood sisters. I don't have a needle, do you?"

Naomi was glad she didn't. Poking your finger hurts. They printed Goodbye, Bird on a white piece of birchbark.

Naomi wonders if the birchbark is still there under the stone where they buried the bird. She hides the card from Mitzi under her pillow.

Stephen is sitting at the table, biting his pencil. He's doing his homework. Obasan is washing the mushrooms.

"So big," Obasan says. "Such fat mushrooms."

Uncle has put the pink rose in a glass tumbler. It's on the table in front of Stephen.

No one is watching as Naomi hunts for a needle in Obasan's sewing box under the bed. There's one with a long black thread on it. She squinches her face up and jabs her pointer finger. Oo! A tiny dot of blood comes out when she squeezes hard.

She takes Mitzi's card from under the pillow. *Bap!* There it is now. Naomi has made a blood blotch too. She takes out her pencil and signs her name.

"It's done! We are sisters and friends for life." Naomi is so happy she plops her face into the pillow and laughs out loud.

Chapter 19

It's early, early in the morning. Where am I? What is this place? Naomi wonders.

Is she having a dream? It doesn't seem like a dream.

Wait. This isn't right, she thinks. She's awake. But she was asleep just a minute ago. She was dreaming about Daddy and Mama and Grandma Kato. It felt as real as the lumpy bed on which she is lying, as real as the sound of the clock *tick, tick, ticking* comfortingly on the shelf.

There's a light hazy glow in the room. She doesn't know where it's coming from. It isn't greyish white like the light from the moon. It's more yellowy. Her head feels funny, as if there's a wind rushing around in it.

Mama was here in this very room. She's sure of it. So was Daddy. And Grandma Kato was sitting in a huge tub of water so hot it was burning red and blue in her dream. *Life is not easy*, Grandma Kato said. Her washcloth was a white square like the cardboard Mitzi sent to Naomi. Grandma was singing quietly and slowly.

How did you Miss Daffodilly
Get your pretty dress?
Is it made of gold and sunshine?
Yes, child. Yes.

Naomi was little in her dream, as tiny as a peach baby. She was so glad to see Grandma and Mama and Daddy. She put out her tiny arms to them.

A match is safe if you can blow it out, Mama said. *There are ways to blow matches out. Even when the world is on fire, there are safe roads to walk on. Find your road, Naomi. I will wait for you on your road.*

And suddenly the water around Grandma was burning. The air was burning. Naomi couldn't move in her dream. Somehow she knew she was dreaming, and she knew her eyes were closed. At the same time, she could see them and she knew she was also awake. Isn't this funny? she thought. I can see Mama and Daddy with my eyes closed.

God's angels are always with you, Daddy said. And then Naomi's eyes opened and she was in the hut in the darkness with Stephen and Uncle and Obasan.

"I know you're here," Naomi whispers as she hugs her pillow. Even if the room is dark, she feels as if she is in a fuzzy golden dream. She is so sure Mama and Daddy and Grandma are still with her, although she can't see them anymore. It's almost like the time she woke up in Slocan and Daddy was on the cot with his back to her.

The clothes are washed and hanging on a line above the stove. The wild rose is on the table. She tiptoes over to sniff the rose. It smells a little like Mama's perfume.

Uncle turns his head as Naomi climbs off the bench. "It's early," he whispers.

"I had a dream," Naomi whispers back and she tells Uncle about it. Uncle sits up, listening carefully and nodding his head. "Mama and Daddy and Grandma—here?" he asks.

Naomi nods.

Uncle lowers his eyes. "Are they still here?" he asks softly.

"I don't know, Uncle," she says.

Uncle stares as if he can see through the walls. Finally he whispers, "Let's pack some food, Naomi."

Obasan opens her eyes. "Too early," she says.

Uncle nods solemnly.

Naomi doesn't know where she and Uncle are going. She puts some bread in a bag as quietly as she can. Uncle fills a bottle with juice from a can.

The sky is still dark except for the stars as they start walking across the field. They pass the swamp. They pass the mushroom patch and the wild roses. They walk on and on over fields and along roads until Naomi says, "I'm tired," and they sit in the slope of the ditch in the cool morning. A small trickle of water is at the bottom of the ditch. From far across the fields, they can hear a rooster crowing. They sit and sit, looking around at the wide, flat land in the darkness.

"I'm hungry," Naomi says at last.

Uncle is looking at the still dark sky. "No one knows," he says quietly. "No one knows. No one knows."

Uncle breaks the bread into pieces for Naomi, and they take turns drinking from the bottle of juice.

When they finish, Uncle says, "*Sa.*" And they start to walk again until they come finally to the long, slow slope of the coulee that goes down and down to the river at the bottom. Uncle puts his hand out and points to the miles and miles of grass quivering gently in the morning breeze and the long shadow of the coulee. "It's like the sea," he says. Naomi thinks about the ripples in the ocean and the lake in Vancouver and Slocan.

Far away to the east, at the beginning of morning and the edge of the world, the clouds are changing red and purple and orange, brighter than fire.

"Mama said, 'Even when the world is on fire, there are safe roads to walk on.' What did she mean, Uncle?" Naomi asks.

"Someday, someday, we will understand," Uncle says softly.

Chapter 20

Many years go by and Naomi becomes an old woman. Stephen is old too. He is a musician who has a piano and a violin, a flute and trumpet, just as he said he would. Mama died in Japan because of the war. Daddy died in a hospital near Slocan. Naomi is like the old woman in the Momotaro story. For her, children are the most precious treasures in the world.

One day Naomi and Mitzi are visiting Vancouver. Mitzi is driving and they are looking for a place to have breakfast. Suddenly Naomi says, "Oh, Mitzi, I used to live near here."

Mitzi says, "Okay, let's go find your old house."

They drive along and drive along. Finally Naomi says, "I think we missed it. Oh well. Too bad." Then she looks on the other side of the street. And there it is! And it has For Sale signs in front!

They both jump out of the car. Mitzi climbs over

the fence and jumps into the yard, even though she is quite old. Naomi laughs. "That's you, Mitzi," she says.

Mitzi pulls open the gate and down the steps they go. The house is just as Naomi remembers it, with lots of windows in the front room where Daddy used to play music. She goes into the backyard and the door to her playroom is also just as it was. The garage is there too. And then, in the very back by the fence, Naomi sees her old cherry tree. She comes up to it and claps her hands to her heart. The tree is scarred and wounded. A bandage is on one branch. Two ropes tie the wounded branch to the trunk. Rusty sap and clear sap seeps through the wounds.

Naomi looks up into the cherry leaves. The tree makes her think of Mama, and the branch that is tied to the trunk makes her think of herself as a little girl, clinging to her. And suddenly the tears she has not cried all her life come pouring out. It is as if Mama has come to meet her and Mitzi here.

You see, she can hear Mama say. *I have come to you on Friendship Road. Welcome home, my special N.*

Naomi's tears are tears of happiness and sadness.

She is laughing and crying at the same time. She puts her arms around the tree. Mitzi puts her arms around Naomi. They look at each other. Then they look up at the sky and smile.

It seems to them that the tree, the branches, the leaves, the air around them and all the creatures in the whole world are smiling and smiling, and everything is just as it was when they were both little girls.

Historical Note

When the war in Europe broke out in 1939, there were approximately 22,000 people of Japanese ancestry living in Canada, most on the West Coast. In 1941, after the Japanese attack on Pearl Harbor in Hawaii, the Americans declared war on Japan and entered World War II. Both Japanese Americans and Japanese Canadians were rounded up and sent to internment camps. Thanks to the American Bill of Rights, however, Japanese Americans were able to return to their homes before the end of the war.

The Canadian government, on the other hand, confiscated the properties of Japanese Canadians. Often with less than twenty-four hours notice, Japanese Canadians were forced to leave their homes. They were fingerprinted and given criminal identification cards. Husbands were separated from their wives and children. For the duration of the war, they were imprisoned in hastily built internment camps deep in the British Columbia interior. They lived in tarpaper shacks unfit for winter, with no sanitation.

The Japanese Canadians' homes and possessions were sold to pay for their internment, making it impossible for them to return once the war was over. The Dispersal Policy resulted in Japanese Canadians being scattered across the country, east of the Rockies, to areas where labour was required. Many, like Naomi's family, ended up in the sugar beet fields of southern Alberta.

Moreover, in 1946 the Canadian government deported 4,000 Japanese Canadians to Japan, thus being the only democratic country to deport its own citizens who were guilty of no crime. More than half of these people were native-born Canadians.

On April 1, 1949, four years after the end of the war, Japanese Canadians were finally granted the rights of citizenship—the right to vote, to work at any job they wished, and to travel where they pleased. Not one Japanese Canadian was found guilty of disloyalty to Canada.

It was not until September 22, 1988, that the

Canadian government officially acknowledged that the wrongful actions were motivated by racism. All Japanese Canadians born before 1949 were awarded $21,000 as a token compensation. No efforts have been made to return their properties.

In August 2003, on the day that Mars was closest to the earth, the author and her friend, Fernande Faulkner, discovered by chance that her childhood home at 1450 West 64th Avenue in Vancouver was still standing and for sale. The Kogawa Homestead Committee, headed by Anton Wagner, launched an effort to preserve the house as a site for friendship and reconciliation. That effort continues.

Michiko Asami, the translator of *Naomi's Road* into Japanese, has been building Friendship Road between Canada and Japan for many years. She and the author share the belief that even one handful of sand on Friendship Road helps to make the world a safer place.

Joy Kogawa

Joy and her older brother Tim in 1937

Joy Nakayama was born in Vancouver in 1935. Like Naomi, the Nakayama family were interned in Slocan, British Columbia and later sent to Coaldale, Alberta after the Second World War. Joy Kogawa taught school in Coaldale then studied for a year in Toronto. She now lives in Toronto and Vancouver. Kogawa is a recipient of numerous honorary doctorates as well as national and international awards for her writing. In 1986 Kogawa was named a Member of the Order of Canada. Her books include four volumes of poetry and three novels: *Obasan, Itsuka* and *The Rain Ascends*. In 2004, the City of Vancouver declared November 6th Joy Kogawa Day. In addition, the Vancouver Opera has commissioned an opera based on *Naomi's Road*.